THE SOMALI DECEPTION

DECEPTION

EPISODE III

DANIEL ARTHUR SMITH

The Somali Deception Episode III
Copyright © 2010-14 Daniel Arthur Smith
All rights reserved Holt Smith ltd
Second Edition
Cover Design and Formatting by Daniel Arthur Smith
Edited by Crystal Watanabe

Published by Holt Smith Limited
ISBN: 0988649357
ISBN-13: 978-0988649354

Also Written by Daniel Arthur Smith

The Cameron Kincaid Adventures
The Cathari Treasure
The Somali Deception

The Literary Fiction Series
The Potter's Daughter
Opening Day: A Short Story

The Horror Series
Agroland

~*~

For Susan, Tristan, & Oliver, as all things are.
&
To all of the others that choose to use crayons to color
their rainbows.

~*~

.

EPISODE III

CHAPTER 41
THE MAY FAIR HOTEL, LONDON, MAYFAIR

Pepe's eyes fixed on his reflection in the stainless steel of the service lift doors. He extended the back of his neck to lengthen his height and then pulled in his gut. He frowned at the result.

"You're just now noticing," observed Cameron. He peered at his own reflection. He raked his fingers above his ears through the wafts of hair that appeared to hold more grey than when he had left New York only days before. "We're all getting older."

Pepe slid his hands to the inside of his grey sport coat. He hoisted his trousers and then smoothed his maroon mock turtleneck above his waist. He patted his belly in place and then smirked at his faux thinner appearance. "Speak for yourself."

"I'll have you know I run every morning and hit the gym every night," said Cameron. "I have to be in shape for the cameras, at least. You can't tell me you still run."

"I am as fit as ever," said Pepe. "No, I don't run. I

still do my katas though, and yoga now, too."

Cameron lifted one brow. "You do yoga?"

"Yes, yoga," said Pepe, indifferent to Cameron's skepticism. "Keeps me limber," he paused, then added, "For the ladies."

Cameron grinned.

Pepe shrugged. "Too much food on the plane is all. Every plate is served American now."

"Now that is cognitive dissonance."

"Guh," said Pepe. "You know, I think he should have come anyway. His connections here in London could have been useful."

Cameron flexed his head to one side and then to the other. "I would have liked Alastair to come as well. Heading back to Kenya was a good idea, though. He can work with Eazy to trace back the satellite imagery from the time of the hijacking. If we would have done that rather than following the false intel we would—"

"I know," said Pepe. "We would have her by now."

"Besides, Alastair is Kenyan. We have as many connections here as he does, easily. We have all of the connections we need." Cameron readied the SIG P226 9mm hidden beneath his jacket, making sure not to reveal the handgun to the camera in the upper corner of the cabin. "We are almost there."

"I'm ready," said Pepe. He hoisted the small black nylon duffel from the floor between them, swinging the bag up to his side to swallow his other hand.

The doors to the service lift opened onto the fourth floor, the luxury level containing many of the May Fair Hotel's illustrious suites. The two were explicitly there to revisit the Amber suite. Though the décor of the May Fair corridor was the same as their last visit days before, the same carpet, same wall covering, same indirect artificial candlelight, their intent brought a new vibrancy to the place. Abbo Mohammed's last words were that Ibrahim Dada was behind the Seychelles hijacking of the Kalinihta, behind Christine's abduction. If what Abbo told them were true, then this visit would play out much differently than the last.

The service lift opened to a hidden alcove near the stairwell at the end of the corridor. The lift bay for the hotel guests Cameron and Pepe had arrived in on their prior visit was at the opposite end of the hallway and from there, halfway down the adjacent corridor, was the Amber suite.

Cameron and Pepe acted with a sense of urgency, their strides rhythmic and their motion direct. Hammers ready to strike nails.

As they rounded the corner of the corridor, Cameron removed the Sig P226 from under his jacket. The same titan was guarding the suite, his posture impressively statuesque, unwavering. Cameron was impressed that the mammoth man, after peripherally dismissing their first steps, snapped toward a defense pose with such immediacy. The nimble sentinel appeared more machine than organic. The guard's impressive defensive move was no matter, however. The micro second hesitation was enough for the MP5 inside of Pepe's nylon duffel to release two bursts. The massive bodyguard slammed to the carpeted floor before gaining his stance.

Crossing the front of the door without losing stride, Pepe slapped a sticky charge on the area where they had seen the added interior locks. Stopping short of the door, Cameron slipped his forged keycard into the lock slot, and then added a second sticky charge below. Both men pressed their backs firmly against the wall and glanced away. The sides of the door above and below the lock slot disintegrated in a loud thud. Cameron pulled the security keycard back out of the lock slot. The small scarlet LED blinked out, the emerald light went on, and no alarms were triggered downstairs.

Pepe threw his hand down on the latch. Cameron swung a barrelhouse kick into the door.

There was a loud crack and then the sound of thunder.

The door bluntly slammed onto the second titan, forcing him back into the wall. The sawed off shotgun he held met his chest, and erupted into his shoulder.

The large man howled.

Pepe immediately took his place to the front of Cameron. He was well past the door when, still pinned against the blood-spattered wall, the giant's body buckled. As Cameron passed the mangled guard, his sinuses filled with the hot metal odor of the newly spent shotgun shell, and the pungent urine soaking the whimpering man's clothes.

Cameron jabbed the door again. With another howl, the giant collapsed to his knees.

For the second time, Pepe and Cameron entered the heart of the large beige and brown luxury suite. The objects d'art and many amber lamps in the room were still the same, yet as the corridor, the Amber suite had changed.

In the center of the large L-shaped amber plush sofa sat Ibrahim Dada, in his impeccable Savile Row tailored suit, appropriately the centerpiece of the room. Despite the shotgun blast and howls from the hallway, the well-groomed dark African again appeared indifferent to Cameron and Pepe entering the room. A football match, different teams from the last visit, was in play on the plasma television.

Apart from Dada, the room was clear. Pepe and Cameron were silent, their weapons drawn toward the warlord statesmen.

A long moment passed and nothing happened, not even on the screen. The players volleyed the ball to and fro and nowhere, meandering around the field.

From the couch came a long tired sigh, almost a yawn, yet somehow more polite. Then Dada carefully pinched the knees of his trousers and lifted himself from the sofa. He slowly turned from the television to Cameron and Pepe and said, "A dull game, really, wouldn't you say?"

4

Cameron and Pepe said nothing.

"Gentlemen, there was no need for all of the fuss. You are welcome here, particularly since I seem to be in your debt."

"We wanted your attention, Mister Smith," said Pepe.

"Or should we call you General Dada?" asked Cameron. "Or do you go by Admiral now?"

"Well, many titles, actually. As I mentioned to you the last time you visited, I am in this country on diplomatic status. Anyway, as we appear to know each other now, let's say we cut the formality, Mister Kincaid. May I call you Cameron?"

"Kincaid will be fine."

"Then call me Dada."

CHAPTER 42
THE MAY FAIR HOTEL, LONDON, MAYFAIR

Pepe and Cameron were in a state of war. They were on a mission. The mission was direct action infiltration and exfiltration, objective one being to secure and rescue Christine Laroque, and if she was not in the suite, then objective two was to identify her location.

Neither Cameron nor Pepe were pure soldiers anymore. Neither lived the constant rigor that was a lifestyle yet also the mental fortification that kept them bound to honor. Since neither man was as they once were, each was beginning to deal with the toll of the last few days in a different way.

Cameron kept using the crutch of rationalization for his actions and he was well aware that his old friend Pepe was becoming a new man altogether. Pepe would not be burdened with rationalization and that would ultimately lead to something vacuous, of pure blind intent. Cameron understood that Pepe was distinguishing civility from direct action less and less by each hour, becoming an untempered

6

lethal force that would not hesitate to consider anyone in the way of his mission expendable or collateral damage. They had both been trained to know when to put blinders on and when to create a two-color world. Cameron was not compartmentalizing when he took his blinders off and Pepe was leaving his on. Cameron and Pepe needed to find Christine soon, for their sake as well as hers.

Before Cameron and Pepe was Ibrahim Dada, deceivingly groomed in the fashion of a wellborn patrician, far in manner and creature comfort from the pauper fisherman that had turned to fighting early in his country's civil war. Appearing calm, cool, metered, and indifferent, Dada was as deceiving in manner as the whole of Somali piracy. No wonder that no westerner understood the core of Somali piracy, marketed to the western world as simple-minded marauders driven by greed.

There were those evil men, simpleton thugs and rapists, abducting tourists and aid workers for unheard of ransoms. They were gangsters no different than the kidnapping bands of thieves of South and Central America, or the street clans that owned the shadows and slums of every global city.

True piracy was something else, something so much larger, on a far greater scale. Men such as Ibrahim Dada did not conduct their business alone. They held seats at the table, with men and women educated at Harvard, Oxford, Cambridge, and Yale. They parleyed with officers of major corporations and financial institutions, modern day corporate aristocrats that by all but description were pirates themselves. Men such as Ibrahim Dada held court with those that shared a vision, a grand vision. In them, he saw himself grand, immaculate, impeccable, and though that is how Ibrahim Dada portrayed himself and believed himself to be, to Cameron he appeared otherwise. As through the psychologist's Johari window, where part of the subject is hidden to himself and revealed to others, Dada appeared to

Cameron as the true sociopath he was, a psychopath without empathy, remorse, or trepidation. The flawless Savile Row suit tailored to fit Ibrahim Dada clothed a monster, not a man.

"You wasted no time coming from Dubai," said Dada. "You must be thirsty."

Dada walked slowly to the side bar. "I would offer you food as well," he gestured toward the hallway, "but unfortunately I am a bit understaffed at the moment."

"It was you that hijacked the Kalinihta," said Cameron.

"Now, let's see," Dada clasped his hands together, "what do we have? Honestly, I have not had to make a libation for myself in quite some time."

"Why did you lie to us?"

"Here we go, what would you like? Gin, whiskey, American bourbon, perhaps?"

The black nylon duffel let loose a short burst.

The lamp at the end of the sidebar shattered.

"We are not here to drink," said Pepe.

A veteran of combat, Dada did not flinch. "Your choice," he said. "I will have a bourbon." Dada lifted a rectangular crystal container from the back of the side bar and removed the cork. "I am not so much a practicing Muslim, really."

"We have an idea of what's going on," said Cameron. "We wanted to hear it from you."

Dada faced them and lifted his newly poured rock glass to his chest, letting the index finger of his other hand lightly surf the rim. He sighed, then said, "What is going on? I tell you, more than you can imagine."

"The girl from the yacht," said Pepe. "You knew we would come for her, now where is she?"

From behind Cameron and Pepe came a deep recognizable voice, "She had a lovely scream, musical."

Cameron and Pepe spun to face each other. They and Dada were still the only three in the room. The voice had come from Pepe's right, through an empty open door in the far corner, behind the long glass-topped dining table. They each eased back toward the walls behind them, Cameron toward the inner wall, still covering an indifferent Dada, and Pepe, backing to the outer wall, focused on the open doorway. When Pepe reached the far wall, he flashed a subtle finger gesture to Cameron to signal that his line of sight through the open door was clear. The owner of the voice within the next room of the suite was behind the wall.

"You remember Colonel Tijon," said Dada. "You have met before."

Cameron was bitter. "We were never properly introduced."

"So beautiful, that one," bellowed the voice. "Trembling and quivering." From the adjoining room the tall bald man, dressed again in his fine white suit, crept partially into the frame of door, his head tilted to the side to make him fit. "I do not know if she had ever seen a black man so large before."

Pepe's lip curled, "You bastard." His right arm shot erect, the black nylon duffel almost falling away. A rapid cascade of holes appeared in the plaster above the incredibly nimble Colonel Tijon as he dove behind the long dining table, his own submachine gun in hand.

Pepe trailed the flying white suit with another immediate burst while simultaneously Tijon sent a volley of bullets up from the floor. Assailed from two directions, the thick lead glass tabletop disintegrated. Pebble sized glass fragments sprayed the entire end of the room.

The P226 in Cameron's hand, unable to target, hovered in an uncertain circle toward the floor behind the table, while Cameron flashed his head over to Dada, and then to Tijon again.

The MP5 extended in Pepe's arm appeared to lead him in a march around the end of the topless table.

Cameron moved toward the table from his side of the

9

room.

In a surreal gymnastic maneuver, Tijon launched a chair toward the MP5, using the momentum to bring himself to his feet. The MP5 dislodged from Pepe's grip. Pepe threw his weight toward the rising man, skullcap first. They connected head to shoulder. Tijon's height and Pepe's girth collided, and both men spun at the opposing force.

Cameron lifted his hand to fire. In his peripheral, Dada was moving away. He spun back toward Dada, who was briskly making his move for the master bedroom.

"Hold on," said Cameron. He bolted behind Dada, not wanting to shoot him. Dada reached the master bedroom. The door swung toward Cameron. His arm extended, Cameron lunged to catch the door, but failed. The door slammed his fingertips. He could hear the metal engage and then click inside of the frame. Cameron still attempted the latch. He thrust his shoulder into the thick solid wood. They had brought no more sticky charges.

"Cut him off, he is going out into the hall," shouted Pepe.

Cameron spun back toward Pepe and Tijon. Fists raised, they were now trading punches. A clue Tijon was educated abroad was that he held a traditional boxing stance. His form was rigid and predictable. Pepe was trained in a variety of martial arts—Taekwondo, Kung Fu, Karate—and he was a Judo master. Pepe had an array of techniques at his disposal, and of the many, he chose to mock Tijon with the Wushu form Zui quan, that of the drunken boxer. Tijon continued to throw blows that could not connect. Even when Tijon dared to be creative, stout Pepe easily out maneuvered him. Pepe dodged an elbow strike that cratered the sidewall, and then returned with a solid uppercut.

Pepe was faring on his own. Dada was the priority.

Cameron realized that of course Pepe was right. Dada would only have gone into the master bedroom if there were a way out, an escape route. He let his brain go calm and hurried to the hallway. The steel doors of the guest lift were already sliding shut.

CHAPTER 43
THE MAY FAIR HOTEL, LONDON, MAYFAIR

The large carcass outside of the Amber suite door reeked from loosened bowels. The sides of Cameron's sport coat spread away from him as he launched over the corpse into a full run down the fourth floor corridor. He did not slow for the corner, or to mess with the guest lift, rather he burst directly through the door of the stairwell and leapt over the steps to the landing below. Cameron took more time spinning around the half flight landings than the short bounds across each set of steps.

At the lobby level, he thrust himself through the stairwell door into a calm and empty hallway. The serenity struck him hard and sent him reeling back to the near wall. He was holding a handgun in a country where he should not have one, and the cameras had only been rigged for the fourth floor. He stilled himself. He remembered stealth. Nonchalantly, Cameron straightened his posture. He slid the P226 beneath his coat and then, with a brisk and study stride, made his way toward the lobby.

Apart from the Clef d'Or concierge, the lobby was empty. The dull grey light of dusk poured in from the street onto the ruby-laden Baccarat chandelier and surrounding eclectic objects d'art transforming the lobby of the finest hotel in London to a sleepy Tuesday evening gallery.

There was no sign of Dada.

Cameron moved first one and then his other foot back before spinning toward the direction he came. He quickened his stride and then with a glance back to ensure no one was watching, eased up to jog the few steps to the stairwell.

Before the stairwell door closed, Cameron propelled himself inside, scrambling from landing to landing, down to the lower level. He suspected he could access the secret sublevel parking structure that he and Pepe had discovered days before from here. The humid service floor was eerily vacant. Giant tumbler dryers whirred around him. Cameron raised his weapon and began to prowl through the narrow spaces between the tall laundry machines.

From the corner of the room he heard the clank of a metal door closing.

Cameron marched toward the corner. He found a door behind one of the mammoth industrial dryers. He loosely clutched the latch, pressed his shoulder to the door, and readied his P226. He began a mental four count and on two, he pushed and released the latch while forcing his shoulder into the door. The door flung open to the garage and found two young men dressed in the garb of May Fair service staff, one holding a spliff, the other a lighter. Their eyes went wide and mouths agape.

"We're on break," said the one holding the spliff.

Cameron's P226 was still raised high. He shifted his eyes from the boys to the expanse of the garage and then back. Both of the boys were fixed on his weapon.

"Maybe our break's over," said the young man holding the lighter.

"Yeah," said Cameron. "I think so." With a side step, he pushed the door open further. He flicked his head at the two and then added, "We have a security issue. You'll be safer inside."

The boys looked at each other. "Safe is good," the boy with the lighter said to the one with the spliff. They nodded at Cameron and then scurried past him into the safety of the laundry room.

Cameron slowly stepped away from the door. He peered deep into the underground garage, this time detecting movement on the far side near the exit. The shining white bonnet of a vintage white Bentley skimmed above the tops of the newer luxury cars in the lot. The car was surely the same vintage white Bentley Cameron had seen on his last visit below the May Fair. The same Bentley he and Pepe thought belonged to the tall bald man and, by relation, to Abbo. Moments ago, he had met the tall bald man, Colonel Tijon, which meant the Bentley belonged to Dada.

Outside, somewhere on the street, was the driver Pepe had hired on their last visit, yet no backup car had been parked underground. They had not missed the detail. They had decided that the budget was light for an expense that, ironically, they had agreed was of unlikely use.

Boosting a car was an option, though that could draw too much attention and odds were that the vehicles parked in this secret lair would all be easily traceable through a LoJack system or, like Cameron's own Mercedes, would simply shut off once reported stolen. He could contact their driver to follow Dada, though that would not really be necessary. There was another way to track the warlord. Pepe's local contacts had access to the London closed circuit camera systems, the London CCTV. To find a vintage black Bentley would probably be close to impossible. Finding a vintage white Bentley in the London vicinity would not be so tough.

Rather than return to the stairwell, Cameron went to the lift. He slid in his keycard to return to the fourth floor luxury suite lrbrl. The depth of the sublevel made his earpiece inefficient, silent, so he did not attempt to speak to Pepe until the lift was clear of the lobby.

"I am on my way back," said Cameron. "Are you still in the suite?"

No answer.

Cameron waited for the slow lift to climb another level to speak again, though he was sure the tech was well clear for reception.

"I'm forty-five seconds out," said Cameron. He was confident that Pepe was still in the suite. Pepe would respond if he had gone to the street. For some reason Pepe was silent.

The P226, having dodged the cameras of the lift, was again in Cameron's hand as the metal doors slid open. Halfway down the silent corridor, the corpse of the massive guardian remained twisted in the same collapsed pose. There were no alarms, bells, or whistles, emanating from the small camouflaged boxes mounted on the ceiling and walls. Only the subtle roars of the football match flowed from the Amber suite.

CHAPTER 44
THE MAY FAIR HOTEL, LONDON, MAYFAIR

The stench at the entrance of the luxury suite was far worse than it had been minutes earlier. The giant behind the door had bled out from his self-inflicted wound and, in course, had released his innards. In the brief instant Cameron took to cross the threshold, his eyes flooded. He made a note to himself to leave through the bedroom as Dada had, and then, remembering that the door was bolted, scrunched his face. Cameron stopped in the hall, his P226 ready to fire and his stomach ready to vomit from the smell of putrid sweet sewage at his back. He mentally repeated the mantra, *In through the mouth out through the nose.*

The roars of the crowd emanating from the surround sound system had escalated due to some play or maneuver Cameron could not see. He gleaned for any sound other than that from the match—walking, shuffling—yet there was nothing.

Pepe could be beyond his line of sight, yet so could Tijon.

The odor behind Cameron was unbearable. His stomach knotted and he caught a wretch in the back of his throat. He had to move. Led by his weapon, he entered the main room.

The room was empty, no Pepe, no Colonel Tijon.

To Cameron's right, the door to the master bedroom, the door Dada used to escape, was closed. To his left, a haze of dust floated above the remains of the dining table and an array of bullet holes and cracked plaster bordered the door from which Colonel Tijon had entered. The carpet between Cameron and the doorway was matted with countless fragments of broken glass from the disintegrated tabletop. He crept toward the open door with all of the stealth he could muster, unable to silence the glass crunching beneath his feet.

Cameron froze, the doorway a mere step beyond.

The adjoining room was quiet. Cameron raised his foot to take another step. Mid-step he heard an abrupt smack of metal slapping against a surface. Far inside the room, something had dropped onto a tabletop. A slow rickety creaking followed. The unmistakable creak of an old desk chair, taking the weight of a stout man, or a tall one.

In a sleek move, Cameron let himself fall forward into the doorway, so that as he spun toward the far side the room, his body was lower than a predicted line of fire.

No weapons were fired.

The walls were marred with blood and indented by strikes from the room's lamps and side chairs, the remnants of which were shattered across the floor. There was a man seated at a desk as Cameron had deduced, Pepe. Colonel Tijon was standing next to the desk, facing the wall. Not standing, Cameron realized, as much as being held upright by his head, which was lodged into the wall. The chair was bent unnaturally back, threatening to collapse under Pepe's weight. Pepe reclined further, twisting the chair to face Tijon. Pepe's sport coat was on his lap, ripped and tattered.

He did not appear to have any cuts yet his knuckles, forearms, and face were scarlet, coated with blood, blood that was not his.

Cameron spoke softly, "We need to get out of here. We have to put a trace on Dada's car."

Pepe did not shift his body or veer from his gaze. He too spoke quietly, "I found a computer." On the desktop next to Pepe was a silver metal laptop, the source of the slam on the desk.

"You need to see the look on his face," said Pepe, "the man that took my sister."

"I think we better just go. I'm surprised no one is here yet."

"We will, first go into the bathroom and take a look at him."

Cameron raised his voice to a strong plea, enunciating his friend's name, "C'mon, Pepe, let's go."

Pepe spun his head toward Cameron. "Kincaid," he screamed, "look at him."

Stunned, Cameron decided that he best do what his friend of many years had requested. He nodded and then stepped into the small bathroom. He was prepared to see Colonel Tijon mounted on the wall, his head the protruding bust of a trophy animal. What he did not expect to see was a bludgeoned, beaten, and swollen mass. After Pepe had thrown Tijon through the wall, he had continued to beat him past the point of death. Cameron surmised Tijon might not even have been conscious to receive the final deadly blows.

Cameron left the bathroom. Pepe had risen from the chair. In one hand he held his black nylon bag, the end torn from the MP5. His jacket was tucked under his other arm, above the computer.

Pepe spoke softly again, "You're right, we should go. I am a mess."

Cameron faced Pepe, a man becoming twisted in

pursuit of his sister.

"What did you do to that man?"

"I gave him," Pepe paused, "I gave him some of what he deserved."

"In the Legion," said Cameron, "we were trained with the highest code. 'In combat, you act without passion and without hate, you respect defeated enemies'. What did you do, brother?"

Pepe tilted his head slightly to the side. His face was blank. Cameron saw no recognition in his friend's eyes, for him or the words. Then Pepe spoke, "Cameron, of all people, I think you understand. They took Christine." Pepe nodded toward Tijon's lifeless body. "That man took my sister."

"I know," said Cameron. "But we took an oath. We are better than them."

"Kincaid," said Pepe. He paused, shifted his gaze to the floor, and then back into Cameron's eyes. "We are not in the Legion anymore."

CHAPTER 45
THE MAY FAIR HOTEL, LONDON, MAYFAIR

Cameron guarded the door of the lobby restroom to ensure no innocent passerby would enter to witness the deluge of blood-mingled water. Pepe was methodically expedient and efficient in scrubbing the sticky sap from his forearms, hands, and face. The brisk water also appeared to calm and rejuvenate him.

"Careful not to get any blood on that counter," said Cameron. "That white marble doesn't look very sealed."

"You really think you need to tell me how to wash away blood?" asked Pepe.

Cameron did not respond. He wanted to forget what Pepe had said upstairs about disregarding the Legion. They would always be associated with the Legion. They may not be active, yet the Legionnaire's Code of Honor forever bound them. They had made a commitment to live life a certain way. To follow a code that adapted to the world in or outside of the Legion. Honor and fidelity was the way of the Legion, and faithfulness to honor, a portion of that doctrine. Cameron could no more believe that Pepe had resigned his loyalty to honor as he would believe that Pepe could desert him, regardless of a few harsh words.

They had been stalwart members of the Green Dragons and the loyalty Cameron dedicated to his friend, his brother, was mutual and absolute, and could not be abandoned. He had to allow for time and conditions, their vow to fight without passion and hate had come years before the men in the suite had taken Christine. He would have to forgive his friend for a moment of frenzy.

Then Cameron was struck with a moment of clarity. He awakened to a revelation that the absolutes placed on faithfulness and honor were not the true cause of this trepidation. The true cause was not so black and white. In the darkness loomed the greater picture, the extraordinary violence, and an unnecessarily high body count. He realized he had been ruminating the last few days. That he could not quiet his mind irritated him. Legionnaires learn that some people could die, and that some indeed should. They learn not to hesitate, for some people warrant action, the bad people. The events of the past few days, the past hour, though extreme and unorthodox, should not have bothered him. Cameron was in an unexplored space, and Pepe, he feared, was cracking, or had already cracked. They were confronting cartel leaders and killing them off like bugs; repercussions were inevitable.

Pepe had finished scrubbing. As Pepe dried his hands, he peered questionably into Cameron's eyes.

"Did you go somewhere?" asked Pepe.

Pepe's jovial tone and expression had returned. The presence of a familiar Pepe snapped Cameron back from distraction. "Huh, yeah. I guess I wandered off."

Pepe smiled and then patted Cameron on the shoulder. "Well, stay close my friend, I need you near me."

From within the black nylon duffel Pepe retrieved a dark grey long sleeved shirt similar to the bloodied maroon one he had folded into his sport coat.

"You brought a change of clothes?" asked Cameron.

Pepe laughed. "No, of course not. This shirt was in a package in one of the bureaus." He pulled the shirt over his head and then pulled the waist in place. He patted his stomach and curled the side of his lip. "Must have been purchased for one of his men," he said.

"Hey," said Cameron. "You look fine. Now let's get out of here. I want to check with your friend to see where the Bentley has gone off to."

"Of course," said Pepe. He gathered his jacket with the bloodied shirt tucked neatly inside, the computer, and his black nylon duffel. The two exited the restroom and slid out the first side door as incognito as possible.

"Taxi, gentlemen?" asked the curbside doorman.

"No, thank you, we are walking this evening," said Cameron. The two began to make their way down Stratton toward Berkeley Street.

Pepe held the nylon duffel out to Cameron. "S'il vous plait."

Cameron took the duffel from Pepe, who began digging through his front pocket for his mobile phone. He fished out the device, perused the screen with his thumb, tapped a name, and then put the phone to his ear.

Cameron tilted his head toward Pepe. "I have been meaning to mention. I noticed you finally gave in on a new phone."

Pepe smirked. "They forced me by discontinuing service on my old one." He nodded his chin toward the device. "This girl, Kincaid, she will know where the Bentley is, guaranteed, and if Dada has left the car, she will know too. She is tuned in to the closed circuit with her computer. Magic is what she does." He raised his arm holding the laptop and made a waving gesture as they crossed Berkeley Street. "Probably watching us now."

Cameron raised a brow. "One of your ladies maybe?"

Pepe raised his brow in return. "My cousin." The tone of Pepe's voice abruptly changed, "Victoria, bonsoir." Cameron and Pepe turned to walk down Berkeley Street. Pepe continued, "Bien, bien." A pause. "Oui, blanc Bentley." Another pause, "Aha, oui." The two men stopped to the side of their waiting car, the black Bentley Pepe had arranged for them on their last visit. Cameron opened the rear door and bowed his head to move inside, and then Pepe stopped him. Cameron straightened and then turned back to Pepe to see why his friend was holding him by the arm. Pepe had the mobile phone between his shoulder and chin. "Oui," said Pepe again softly. He released Cameron's arm to point across the street. Cameron followed the gesture to Pepe's target and there, parked halfway down the block in front of the May Fair Hotel's Palm Beach Casino, was the white Bentley.

"Oui. Merci. Ciao," said Pepe and then he pulled the phone from his ear.

"That is our white Bentley parked outside of Palm Casino?" asked Cameron.

"Yes. She said the car drove around the block to the front of the casino."

"And Dada?"

"She has access to the cameras inside as well," said Pepe. "Dada is in the VIP room in the Palm Beach Casino."

CHAPTER 46
THE PALM BEACH CASINO CLUB, LONDON, MAYFAIR

With the light of day past, the tourists of the Mayfair district had departed. A sparse number of denizens quietly darted up the walk, en route to supper or cocktails. A sconce lit canopy near the back of the May Fair Hotel denoted 'The Palm Beach Casino Club.' Cameron stopped short of the art deco glass doors to glance across Berkeley Street, back toward the Nobu restaurant. In front of the restaurant, parked between a Ferrari and a Maserati, was the Bentley Pepe's friend had arranged a few days prior.

Unable to see into the car, Cameron nodded. "I heard you," he said. "My earpiece is working fine. You can hear me all right, then?"

From the backseat of the Bentley, hidden from Cameron by shadow, Pepe responded, "Loud and clear."

"Okay, here we go," said Cameron. "Let's see if I am remembered."

"The way you part with money, I doubt they would have forgotten the Dragon Chef."

"You don't tire of saying that do you?"

"The phrase pleases me," said Pepe.

Cameron reached for the door. Before he could grip the long handle, the tall glass door began to open. Inside the vestibule, a doorman spread his free arm up to gesture Cameron inside.

"Welcome back to the Palm Beach Casino, Mister Kincaid."

"Thank you," said Cameron as he walked into what once was the grand art deco ballroom of the May Fair Hotel and had since become the most exclusive casino in London.

Comfortably spread out across the room were at least ten roulette tables, a small casino as gambling houses go. Light hued wood, indirect artificial candlelight, a few other games, and some festive gamblers created an effervescent atmosphere.

A second man greeted Cameron as he entered the room. "Welcome, Mister Kincaid," he said. "We are so pleased to have you back."

"Thank you, I'm sure," said Cameron.

A light chuckle resonated in Cameron's inner ear.

"I remind you the maximum bet on the floor this evening is one thousand pounds. What game would please you, sir?"

"Is the Gold Room open?" asked Cameron.

"Excellent, I was about to suggest that. We do have some VIP guests such as yourself in the Gold Room and you are welcome to join them. The game this evening is blackjack."

"That would suit me fine," said Cameron.

"Very good, Mister Kincaid," said the man at the door. A young beautiful brunette woman approached. She was attired in an indigo cocktail dress that appeared more sophisticated than usual for a member of the staff. "Please escort Mister Kincaid to the Gold Room."

"Certainly," said the young woman. She then gave

Cameron an endearing smile. "If you can follow me, Mister Kincaid."

Cameron followed the young woman toward the casino floor. His first step onto the spongy carpet caught him off guard. Cameron sometimes ran on a track at the New York East River Park. The surface of the running track had the same floating push and bounce. He oriented himself, peering around the room, his mindful habit. He glanced to the electronic slot machines lining the outer edges, counting them. There were never more than twenty slot machines in a London casino, a gambling law. They neared the round floor in the center of the room, home to one of the ten roulette tables.

The croupier spun the ball and at the same moment called, "No more bets."

A few young players dressed in high priced jeans and pressed collar shirts continued placing bets even when the ball was rolling. The croupier appeared not to mind. Cameron passed the door to the Poker Room. In the Poker Room, the tables below the palm shaped crystal chandelier were busier than those on the central floor, even busier than the craps game. When they reached the door to the Gold Room, Cameron glanced back across the casino. Something had changed since his last visit.

Cameron mentioned his observation to the young woman. "The baccarat tables that were on the central floor?"

From in his ear Pepe asked, "Is that where you left your money?"

The young woman leaned into Cameron. "Our apologies, Mister Kincaid, games rotate through the casino," she said, and then extended her arm to open the door to the VIP room. She did so in a purposeful maneuver that slid her breasts above the top of her blue dress to his attention. "Can I start you with a beverage?" she asked.

Cameron did not let his eyes fall from hers. "Seltzer

would be nice, with a slice of lime, if you have it."

"Certainly, Mister Kincaid. Would you like me to introduce you to the other guests?"

"That will not be necessary," said Cameron. "Thank you."

Cameron entered the VIP lounge, a smaller room in the fashion of one of the May Fair signature suites and finished with the same light woods as the central casino. There were not many guests in the room. He recognized the two young men on the sofa and the young woman that sat between them; one was a British musician, and the other two were actors. They were drinking pints of lager and watching a football match on the muted plasma television, the same Bang & Olufsen model that Cameron had seen in the Amber suite. In a lounge chair in the corner of the room, a middle-aged man he did not recognize tapped away in a binder, a keyboard and tablet combination. Perhaps the man was a manager to one of the other VIP guests, or merely wealthy.

At the table to the side of the room, a dealer was presenting cards for blackjack. Three of the four seats were filled. Cameron recognized all three of the players, a scruffy British musician from the nineties in mirrored sunglasses, from Manchester if he recalled correctly, an actor from a popular BBC science fiction show, and seated to the side by himself, another man. Ibrahim Dada in his impeccable Savile Row tailored suit gently touched the table to accept or pass cards as they were dealt. Cameron slid the empty chair back enough to sit. Neither Dada nor the musician acknowledged Cameron. The actor met Cameron with a toothy smile. "Hey there," he said. "Yes, do have a seat." The actor then turned back to the cards in front of him and raised his eyebrows. "No need for us to be miserable alone."

"Thank you," said Cameron. "Looks like a good game." A code to Pepe that Dada was at the table as they were told he would be.

"A fourth," said the musician without looking over. "Bloody marvelous, maybe you can change the luck of the table."

Dada said nothing.

The dealer raked in the cards. "Chips, sir?"

Cameron held up his hand spread wide.

"Very good, sir, I can handle that for you," said the dealer. He dropped his arm beneath the table and retrieved a tray of chips with blue and yellow markings along the edges. He rapidly brushed his index finger across them away from his thumb, a bit of motor memory, and then lifted exactly ten chips from the tray.

Cameron placed the stack on the green felt in front of him. "I take it the bet is five hundred?" he asked.

"That is correct, sir," said the dealer.

Each of the others tossed in a chip and the dealer began to place the players' cards face up.

Pepe spoke into Cameron's earpiece, "I have not heard him."

Cameron made a mere grunting noise. The other players paid no notice as the reaction was appropriate, the cards dealt to each totaled to two eighteens, a nineteen, and a twenty. The dealer showed a ten. All four stayed and added another chip, money not being a consequence. In a blink, the table held four thousand pounds of the players' money and still the game was not that interesting. The dealer flipped his hidden card to reveal a three. He drew another card, a king to bust.

"You did bring some luck," said the musician. "This guy has been raking us all night." He gave a nod toward Dada, "Except him."

The actor, jubilant with a win, let the four chips drop onto the felt in front of him in a trickle and then, with his new found luck, immediately tossed two to his betting square.

Cameron tired of Dada's indifference. Less than an hour before, he and Pepe had made mayhem out of Dada's suite upstairs and though the Metropolitan Police sirens had not yet begun to echo through the quaint upscale district of Mayfair, Cameron was certain they would soon. He leaned to Dada and spoke under his breath, "And you, Dada. Do you feel you have luck on your side? The hotel is about to become very hot."

"I do like to gamble," said Dada. "However, I am a diplomat." He flashed a leer to Cameron, "Remember? And this hotel expresses," Dada raised his eyes to the dealer, "the utmost discretion." The dealer peered back knowingly, and then shifted his attention to the deck. "My rooms, I am sure, will be in full repair on my return."

Pepe was noticeably angered, "Listen to him gloat."

"We don't care about your other business or what your," Cameron sucked in a breath through his nose, "*cartel* is doing in London. We want the girl, Dada."

The cards shuffled, the dealer prepared to send out a new round. Dada raised his hand to the dealer. He waved his finger in a circle toward the tall stack of chips. The dealer nodded and then Dada rose from his seat.

"You're leaving so soon?" asked Cameron.

Then from the voice in Cameron's ear, "Let him go. I have his calendar on the computer."

This needed to end now. Ignoring Pepe, Cameron raised himself from his chair, "You really should stay."

"No, Cameron," said Pepe. "He was waiting for reinforcements. Two more sedans have arrived, four men in each. I believe Dada and Abbo recruited every tall man in Somalia."

Dada slowly turned away from the table to Cameron. The warlord's skin was so dark as to be a perfect mask yet his bright eyes, so revealing, made clear his revel of Cameron and the circumstance. "Another dull game," said Dada. "Wouldn't you say?"

Daniel Arthur Smith

CHAPTER 47
CHANNEL TUNNEL, FOLKESTONE, KENT

A blanket of blackness abruptly cloaked the Eurostar cabin car. The English morning was no more. Pepe took no notice, nor did he waver from his task. With the window beside him now gone dark, the train car interior was illuminated by a methodical patchwork of soft hued lights. Pepe appeared frozen against the tall tan leather headrest that spanned the top of his chair. On the small table in front of him, two MacBook Pros traded images, the actions reflecting on the lens of his glasses. One computer was his and the other was from Dada's suite.

Cameron sat across from Pepe in the aisle seat. Their four-club table was the first in the cabin. He leaned to the aisle side of his own cushioned chair so as to split his view between Pepe and the other first class occupants. He stared at the cover of the paperback on the corner of the table. The book he had found at his seat was titled Agroland. The synopsis intrigued him, horror in the Jordanian desert, yet he was too anxious to read. He rested his hand on the cover of the book and then ran his fingertips lightly across the surface in a rapid succession, two then three times, and then recoiled his hand to his lap. He shifted his view to the monitor's reflection in his friend's glasses, admiring Pepe's diligence.

"How many times have you gone through the files on that thing?" asked Cameron.

"A few, we have twenty minutes more in the tunnel and then less than two hours to Paris," said Pepe. "I will keep looking until I can find a clue as to where he is staying, or at least where he is holding her."

"Hmm," said Cameron. He tilted his head toward the aisle and ran his eyes the length of the cabin car. "Any chance he is on the train?"

Pepe dropped his head slightly to peer above the rim of his glasses.

"Only asking," said Cameron, still scanning the occupants of the cabin not hidden from him by the large luxury seats. "He is obviously not here in business premier." He allowed a sneer to push his lips to one side. "I cannot imagine a man like Dada riding coach."

Pepe had returned his attention to the computers, his hands drifting from one to the other as he recorded any findings from Dada's into his own. "He has two entries for today, Eurostar, and dinner in Paris, and for the day after tomorrow lunch at La Closerie de Lilas."

"Times would have been helpful."

"He did not use the calendar program," said Pepe. "The document is an itinerary really, with this week's dates, and those few entries."

"Hmm."

"Besides, he could be on any train," said Pepe, his eyes unwavering from his task, his tone flat. "Or he could have taken the shuttle with his Bentley."

"That's a thought," said Cameron. "Would be a bit easier to find him in Paris." Turning toward Pepe, Cameron straightened a bit. "Speaking of which, do you have any cousins in Paris that have access to the closed circuit camera system?"

"Like in London? No, I do not. Paris is somewhat dark to us in that way. We will have to rely on the street. I have many cousins there."

"Yeah, I remember," said Cameron, settling back to his former position. "I'm sure that'll be fine."

Cameron continued to peer down the length of the aisle at everything and nothing in particular, pensively nibbling his lower lip. The glass door at the opposite end of the car slid silently open, allowing a young blonde woman in a tight fitting Eurostar service uniform to enter pushing a small food and beverage cart. The steward prepared a tea service and then began to offer passengers refreshments. Each time the young woman leaned into a club table or side chair, Cameron lurched a bit to see if the occupant of the seat had changed since he had walked through the car moments before. Of course, the occupants were as they had been, the older couple by the door, the German family at the four-club, and the array of middle and senior managers with their laptops open. Each kind service the same, a recognizable face, the tea and biscuits, and then on to the next, accompanied by a jolt from somewhere within.

Pepe did not need to move his eyes away from the tabletop to sense Cameron's uneasiness. "What's bothering you, mon ami?"

Cameron was quick to respond, "About last night."

"What about last night?" asked Pepe. "She was not there. She will be with him." Pepe's fingers began to rapidly tap the keyboard of his MacBook Pro.

"A bit extreme, don't you think?"

"Oh, the Colonel," Pepe cleared his throat, "Oui." He kept his gaze fixed forward and continued his quest through the computer folders.

"Yes, the Colonel," said Cameron, "the hotel, the hotel

in Dubai, we aren't soldiers anymore."

"I think we did fine," said Pepe. "Maybe you are getting slow."

"That's not what I mean. I did my stint. I live a different life now."

"Maybe you are getting soft."

"Maybe," said Cameron.

"What do you want?" asked Pepe. "Do you want to go back to New York, to your Green Dragon restaurant?" Even with this, Pepe did not make eye contact with Cameron. "Fine, fly out of De Gaulle."

"That's not what I am saying either." Cameron leaned into the table and in a softer voice said, "Pepe, we are not mere killers, we are men of honor."

"Ah, you are still upset about our conversation in Dada's suite," said Pepe, and then he enunciated each of the next words he spoke with a deliberate pause between each, "You are getting soft." Pepe tapped out a few more keystrokes and then in a droll tone added, "Yes, we took an oath. Yes, we are better than them, and you and I, and the others, will always be Dragons together." He slipped off his glasses and gazed kindly at Cameron. "Are you pleased now?" he asked. "You should not have tried to make such a silly point right after I mounted that monster to the wall."

Cameron rubbed the side of his jaw and then squeezed his fist around his chin. "I sound like an old man?"

"You do," said Pepe. He fit his glasses back to his face and returned to the keyboard.

"What are you typing up?"

"I have found spreadsheets with ships and manifests."

"And currency amounts?"

"Neatly beside each ship," confirmed Pepe. "Some in pounds, some in dollars based in percentage by tonnage."

"So it seems that Abbo was not lying about the toxic disposal in Somali waters," said Cameron.

"So it seems, and these numbers add up to large sums."

Pepe spun the computer to Cameron. "Here is another spreadsheet. Does the list look familiar?"

"Yeah, I recognize most of the names, those are the hijacked ships we read about on the way over from New York. This is robust, names, flags, crew complements, cash sums, everything you would need to know to—"

"To hijack a ship," said Pepe.

"Yeah, to hijack a ship. I wonder, do the coordinates in the second column and the dates in the third and fourth column matchup with the hijackings."

"Look at the SS Oceana."

"SS Oceana, here she is, dated—"

Pepe spun his laptop around beside Dada's so that Cameron could see what he had brought up. On the screen was a news article. "Dated yesterday," said Pepe, "The SS Oceana was hijacked yesterday in the Gulf of Aden at the coordinates listed on the spreadsheet."

Cameron pulled Dada's computer closer. "This is list is ongoing. The next ship is dated a few days from now and the next two the week after that."

"The date on the file precedes the date beside the first ship," said Pepe.

"Excuse me?"

"This spreadsheet was made before any of these ships were taken," said Pepe.

"That means—" Cameron rolled his eyes up to Pepe.

"That means all of those ships were scheduled to be boarded," said Pepe. "The dates in the fourth column the planned release date, and the sums in the fifth the prearranged ransom."

"All held for different times and different amounts."

"Insurance limitations, I suppose." Pepe tapped two fingers to the top of the monitor. "I found another spreadsheet that list manifests, arms, chemicals, drugs, all there."

"Dada has come a long way from hoarding

35

international aid. I am surprised he left the May Fair without this."

"I'm not," said Pepe. "The files were in folders that sync with a mobile device. He probably does not realize these were left on this machine."

"So Dada is running the naval operation with a mobile," said Cameron.

"Apparently," said Pepe. He hooked his monitor with his finger and drew the computer back to him. "In the luxury of London. I'm sure Abbo was doing the same."

Cameron tossed his head back onto the leather pillow of the chair. He gazed up at the ceiling. "Dada wasn't even muddled in the casino. He sounded so sure that the rooms would be in order on his return."

"Well, he is a diplomat. I heard him remind you."

"Still, the fact remains that the hotel, or whoever, is in compliance." Cameron slowly shook his head side to side.

Pepe peered over the rim of his glasses again. "And we have never been followed by a clean team?"

"I know, I know, but that was different, those jobs were sanctioned." Even as the words left Cameron's mouth, he realized the hypocrisy. Pepe subtly nodded.

CHAPTER 48
PLACE DAUPHINE, PARIS

The Renault taxi stopped short of the famed restaurant, Caveau du Palais, one of Cameron's favorites in Paris. Cameron stepped to the curb and let Pepe pay the driver. From the inside of the café, the tinny voice of a radio announcer carried out to the street. Over the top of the cab, Cameron could see locals playing pétanque on the sand gravel square among the chestnut trees. In turn, they tossed metal balls toward a wooden one, half the size. Cameron remembered the name of the little ball was the cochonnet, or the piglet. He had played himself in his early days in Paris, and in Corsica where some of the men called the game bouchon.

In the days of playing pétanque, Cameron had not resided in upscale Place Dauphine. He and Pepe had shared leave in a small hotel outside of the city center, in the suburb of Asnières-sur-Seine. At the time, Asnières was still predominantly populated by Pieds Noirs, those French citizens that had lived in northern Africa before the wave of independence. The hotel proprietor, Absolon, had been a Legionnaire as a young man and had then stayed on in

North Africa to build his fortune as a colonist. He was sympathetic to Legionnaires and they received a hotel rate fitting of young soldiers. The constant presence of the young Legionnaires in the hotel reminded the older man of the finer days abroad. Over dinner, the nostalgic hotelier would inevitably switch from wine to cognac and begin to share stories of the Algerian golden era, often crowning the evening singing the unofficial anthem of the Pied Noir, Le Chant des Africains, The Song of the Africans.

In those early days, the young soldiers had caroused through Paris with Pepe's sister Christine and her entourage of friends. Later, when Christine and Cameron became entwined, he shared her small romantic flat near the American University, steps from the Eiffel Tower.

Cameron absently glanced over his shoulder, expecting to see the Eiffel Tower of his youth, only to see the restaurant front of Caveau du Palais.

Pepe exited from the other side of the taxi and faced the square. Before joining Cameron on the curb, he set his duffel on the ground, slid his hands into his pant pockets, and stilled himself in the middle of the street so that he too could take in the Parisians. The moment was picturesque to Cameron; Pepe was standing with his back to him, his satchel squeezed tight under the arm of his sport coat, his duffel beside him, a man returned home. Cameron was unsure what Pepe was thinking for that long moment alone in the street. He imagined his friend was also reminiscent of time spent with Christine. Awake from his brief spell, Pepe slowly joined Cameron at the curb. Without looking back at the square, he said in a low monotone, "You know Place Dauphine has always been my favorite square in Paris. Come, let's have a coffee."

"A pied-a-terre in Place Dauphine among Paris' most beautiful townhouses," said Cameron. "I had no idea you were doing that well."

"Like most here, we inherited a family flat. My aunt

had no children of her own. It is Christine's flat really."
Pepe clutched the top of a café chair of the nearest sidewalk
table. "Let's sit. You will like the espresso. The food and
wine is also excellent. No need to come here if you can't get
a table outside, though."

Cameron inhaled deeply through his nose. That
Christine would live here made sense to him. She was, after
all, a top model with her own wealth. "I would rather go
right up if you don't mind."

Pepe released the chair and raised his brow. "Sure
thing. Let's get right to business." He subtly nodded his
head. "Give me just a moment, I will get the keys and have
them send up some soup and croissant."

"Thank you," said Cameron.

Pepe went to the counter of the café, spoke quickly
with the host, and then rejoined Cameron.

Pepe bent his head back slightly, gesturing to a building
to the right of the restaurant.

"The flat is in the building over, above the gallery."

"Her roommate is expecting us?"

"I spoke with her briefly," said Pepe. "She is on a
shoot in Jakarta."

"She is also a model?"

"Oui," said Pepe. He led Cameron to the forest green
double doors. From his pocket he pulled a key ring. He
stuck an odd shaped key into the lock, sending the door ajar.
With the next key, Pepe unlocked the interior door, a
frosted glass pane etched with an elaborate floral design and
bordered in polished oak. The two proceeded into the small
marble floored lobby. To their right was a set of eight
mailboxes and in the rear, the door to the gallery, a spiral
stairwell, and an open-air lift. They took the stairs to the flat
three stories above. On each landing they passed were three
matching doors, wooden and frail with age. At the top of
the stairs, unique from the others below, was a single dark
saffron metal door. Three shining brass deadbolts lined the

edge. Pepe shook the key ring open into his palm so that the keys to the deadbolts would reveal themselves, and then he methodically unlocked each one.

CHAPTER 49
PLACE DAUPHINE, PARIS

The door to Christine's apartment opened to the bright glow of daylight, enhanced with the contrast of the darkened stairwell. The design of the apartment, far more than a mere pied-a-terre, spoke of Christine. The large flat had been redone in recent years, the smooth ivory walls showed no signs of age and the furniture was new and modern, with the exception of a few choice pieces such as the stuffed tan leather chair and an antique lamp with a Tiffany type art nouveau colored glass shade. The tall, sheer, cloud white panels that draped the windows brought a glow into the room, revealing far behind them the sparse tops of the chestnut trees in the open square below.

The two set their bags near the stairwell that led to the top floor bedrooms. Then Pepe removed the satchel that held the laptops from his shoulder and placed the bag on a small black lacquered table at the end of the sofa. Cameron paced slowly into the vast room. On the sidebar near the door, a piece of china, the pink landscape pattern ancient and dulled, held some euros, a keychain, and a few small folded sheets of paper, pocket worn and discarded, fragments of Christine's day-to-day life. Across the room was a gas fireplace framed with a lacquered cabinet and mantel in fashion with the side tables. A picture atop the mantel caught Cameron's eye. He moved closer; it was a photograph of Pepe and him when they were very young, and each with their arms around a younger stellar beauty, Christine. The three were smiling.

"I remember that day," said Pepe behind him. He was in an open closet reaching for something up top. "That was the day you took her to get the hound. What was that dog's name?"

"Moby," said Cameron.

"Oui, Moby. A silly name for a dog, the name of a whale."

"Immense amour."

"Qua?"

"Christine said the puppy had immense amour, a Moby heart." Cameron lifted the photo from the mantel then glanced up toward Pepe. "She said the dog had an immense love like me."

Pepe nodded solemnly, then raised a hard plastic case he had retrieved from the closet. "Come with me to the table."

Cameron returned the photograph home to the mantel, peered into the picture one last time, and then joined Pepe in the next room. Pepe had placed the case on the table and was working a combination to unlock the lid. Cameron knew what the contents of the case would be and was not surprised when Pepe removed two pistols.

Pepe held one of the handguns out to Cameron. "If I remember, you like a Ruger," he said.

"What's not to like," said Cameron. He pulled the slide back to inspect the P95 and to ensure the chamber was clear. "Center fire, balanced to be ambidextrous," he tossed the Ruger from one palm to the other. "A fine weapon overall." He then picked up the two Ruger magazines bound together by a rubber band and inserted one into the grip. "Besides, I don't think I have much choice. I can't imagine you would give up your M9."

Pepe was inspecting the Beretta he held with the same expedient efficiency as Cameron had with the Ruger. "I also have a SIG 9 in the bedroom closet if you prefer."

Cameron squinted, "You know, I keep only one of these around. In my safe, no less, you seem to have access to a private armory in every western country."

Pepe pulled the slide of the Beretta. "Of the many things a man can do to excess, he can never be too well armed." He handed Cameron a knife from inside the case and then headed up the stairwell. "I will get the SIG."

The intercom near the door buzzed.

"Can you get that?" Pepe's raised voice carried through the flat from the upstairs bedroom. "I am sure that is the food. They were to send up mushroom soup and lamb. You will enjoy the soup."

"And the lamb?" asked Cameron as he went to answer the intercom.

"You will especially enjoy the lamb."

On the black and white screen of the intercom, Cameron watched the slightly doubled image of a young man lift the bags of food up to the camera. Cameron tapped the button to grant the deliveryman access, opened the steel door, and waited for the food to make the journey up the stairs. The echo of the young man's rapid steps shot up the spiral stairwell. He reached the floor in seconds. The deliveryman nimbly stepped across the landing to the door, his thin frame almost swaying from his expedient momentum. Cameron exchanged the euro bill he held out between his fingers for the delivery.

"Merci," said the young man, before spinning around to depart as rapidly as he had arrived. The deliveryman was already a lean shadow descending the first few steps of the spiral stairwell before Cameron was back into the flat.

Cameron walked the box and two large bags over to the table. "What all did you order? This is heavy."

"Must be the wine," said Pepe returning to the table. "They are also very generous."

Pepe opened one of the bags and removed two small paper cups. "Here, have an espresso."

"Thanks," said Cameron. He popped the plastic cover from the lid and then went to the window to again gaze at the square. He sipped the coffee and allowed his eyes to wander from the trees of the square to the street below. "I don't believe this."

"I told you the espresso was good."

"No, yes, but no," said Cameron. "That's not what I meant."

"What is it?"

"There is a white Bentley parked outside."

CHAPTER 50
PLACE DAUPHINE, PARIS

Pepe continued to remove items from the bags. "That has to be a coincidence, we couldn't be so lucky," said Pepe.

"You're right," said Cameron. "How could Dada find us? He could not have followed us all the way from London. Unless." Cameron swung his head in the direction of the satchel. "Could that laptop be bugged?"

"Not really," said Pepe. Then he stopped sorting through the bags and fixed his eyes on Cameron. "Unless it is, location software is standard on Macs."

"Location software?"

"Yes, it is called 'find my computer or phone' or something. That is why I had the old phone you joke about." Pepe shook his head and went back to the bags. "The computer would have to be open though. That is not Dada."

"Unless he followed us," said Cameron.

"You said yourself he could not have followed us from London. Ridiculous." Pepe opened a piece of foil revealing four warm loaves and held them close to his face to take in the sweet scent of the warm bread.

45

"He could have followed us from the Gare du Nord when we left the Eurostar," said Cameron. "You had the computer open on the train."

Pepe lowered the foil-covered loaves and peered up at Cameron. "They could have done this, yes. Tracked us the entire journey with the software and then waited for us at the train station." He shook his head. "It is not them though. We have only arrived."

"They're driving away," said Cameron. The side of his upper lip went up in disgust of his own paranoia. He tilted the paper cup up to pour the rest of the espresso down his throat.

"I told you. Not as many Bentleys in Paris as London, yet still a few." Pepe held his hands above his shoulders. "I asked them to send up some wine. There is no wine here."

Cameron set the paper cup on the table. "I want to stretch my legs anyway. I'll run down."

"Fine," said Pepe. "I will get the plates from the kitchen and you can go downstairs to get the wine. Vin rouge s'il vous plait."

"Of course," said Cameron.

Cameron picked up the SIG Pepe had set on the table and tucked the pistol into his waist opposite the Ruger. "I will be right back," said Cameron. He flashed his brow at Pepe and his old friend returned the gesture.

"Go then, be quick," said Pepe. "Once I open the box the lamb shanks will be cold."

Cameron slipped down the spiral stairwell with the same speed as the young man and was almost to a run exiting the lobby. He caught and composed himself before putting foot on the sidewalk. The white Bentley that had been parked near the restaurant was now nowhere in sight. As he walked the few short meters to the restaurant, Cameron focused his memory on the Bentley. In his mind, he created a still photograph. Cameron studied the picture. The occupants had been out of view from the window above. He ran his eyes along the side of the vehicle and let them rest on the license plate. The country of origin was the UK. Still, he was not sure if the id on the plate had been Dada's. Cameron had been quite far away. He sucked in a deep breath to release the thought, a confused fixation, and made his way through the tables toward the host.

The host recognized Cameron immediately. "Votre ami a oublié le reste de la nourriture," said the host.

"What do you mean my friend forgot the rest of the food?"

The host held up his hand, "Un moment." He stepped over to the counter and returned with two bottles of wine in one hand and a small box in the other. "The young man did not take the lamb." The man smiled as he held the bottles out for Cameron. "I tried to catch him but he was back in the auto and vroom."

Cameron's adrenalin pumped up. "What auto?"

"You did not see?" The host looked confused. "Your young friend has a nice white Bentley, antique I would guess, I tried to get his attention, then vroom." He raised his brow apologetically then again offered the wine and box of lamb. "Your food."

"Merci," said Cameron. Cameron spun around, intent on notifying Pepe back in the flat. Behind him, the further confused host raised his voice, "Your food."

Cameron yelled without glancing back, "Un moment." The Bentley did belong to Ibrahim Dada, there was no doubt, and whatever was in the box under the bags was imminent danger.

The bomb that had been delivered to the fourth floor ignited before Cameron reached the building.

A firestorm bellowed out of the windows of Christine's apartment.

Objects and flame shot out onto the street and into Place Dauphine. The glass of the windows above and below the fourth floor shattered, as did the huge street level pane of the gallery.

The blast was strong enough to disorient Cameron four floors below and threw him into a spin. He landed backward onto the curb to brief silence.

Cameron was in disbelief. People ran out of the Caveau du Palais to the commotion. The street side café was in disarray and the patrons that had been sitting on the walk crawled or hid among the tables and tossed chairs, confused and in shock. A woman was screaming, yet her hysterics were muffled and far away.

The air flooded with rancid smell of the burning building.

Pepe was not running out. Pepe would not be running out.

Years of training kicked in. Stunned and unaware of his own actions, he clutched the Ruger that had fallen to his side, unaware if anyone had noticed. He was unsure how long the 9mm was on the curb, seconds or minutes. Cognizance began to return swiftly with the full caliber of the sounds and smells around him. Cameron scooted himself to his feet. The sirens were very close. Cameron remembered, the police, the hospital, were all only a street or two up the island. He realized he could not be seen there, someone would recognize him in too short of time. He slid the pistol into his jacket and began to casually walk across the square.

CHAPTER 51
PARIS, FIFTEEN YEARS BEFORE

Pepe was elated to see the wee chocolate lab rolling on the blanket next to Christine. He did not bother to acknowledge Cameron or his sister and instead immediately knelt down between them and planted his face close to the frolicking puppy. Moby responded to Pepe as well, leaping toward Pepe's shaking nose with little tiny paws and a nipping jaw.

"He thinks your face is a toy," said Christine.

Pepe behaved no different than Christine had with the small animal, speaking in a childlike way as if Moby were a human baby and not a puppy, "You're a cute little one. Oui, vous êtes."

"How did you find us?" asked Cameron.

Pepe answered Cameron with the same cooing voice, aiming the words at Moby would. "I went by the flat on Rue de l'Exposition and you two were not there. I knew you would be over here at the Champ de Mars, off the field in your spot."

"So I guess there is no hiding from you, mon ami," said Cameron. He rolled back, propping himself up from behind with his elbows. He peered up at a nearby treetop capped with the peak of the Eiffel Tower. The Tower, halfway down the field from where they picnicked, did not appear as large as when viewed from other parts of the city.

Christine gently placed her hand upon the lab's neck. She caressed his delicate shoulders, prompting the puppy to curl into a tight ball. His eyes closed and he appeared to drift to sleep.

Pepe pushed his hands into his knees and straightened his back. "You seem to have a special touch. I think maybe my neck is tight as well." He twirled his head to adjust his neck. The muscles in his upper arms slightly rippled, swelled, and fell with his motion. "Could I be next?"

Christine giggled softly. "You are a big pup yourself, maybe?"

"Really," said Pepe, now exaggerating stretches from his shoulders, "I could use a massage." His tight grey t-shirt accentuated his muscular upper body.

"Then I suggest you go get one," said Cameron.

Pepe stopped his stretching. "I think I will stay. Would I be correct you have some vin rouge in that basket? Maybe some bread?"

"Sure," said Cameron. He lifted the basket over to the side of the blanket where Pepe knelt.

"You are always eating," said Christine. "You should be careful you do not become a huge plum."

"Nonsense," said Pepe. He tore off the heel of a small loaf of bread. "Un quignon de pain ne va pas me faire de mal." He ripped away a piece of the heel with his teeth and then reached into the basket for one of the small bottles of wine to wash the bread down. With a full chewing mouth he said, "I will always be thin and strong." He puffed out his chest and smiled widely, the chunks of bread in his mouth pushing out his cheeks.

Christine laughed aloud.

Pepe shuffled through the basket to find what other

treats were hidden inside. He brought out a silver camera and pointed the lens at his sister. "Let me take your picture." Cameron and Christine leaned into each other. Christine assumed a trained pose and Cameron grinned mildly at Pepe.

There was a click and then Pepe lowered the camera. "That's no good," said Pepe. "Don't be so shy, Cameron. You are with a professional."

Christine turned her head and nuzzled the side of Cameron's face. They both began to laugh.

"Perfect," said Pepe. The camera clicked again. "Now one with the hound."

Christine smugly pushed her lips up and swatted her brother's knee. "Moby is not a hound," she said.

"Excusez-moi, s'il vous plaît pardonnez," said Pepe.

"How about we get a picture together," said Cameron. "Let's ask that man by the tree."

CHAPTER 52
ILE DE LA CITÉ, PARIS

Cameron squeezed his hands into his hips. His blood still pumped hard. He darted his eyes across place du Parvis-Notre-Dame, scanning for anyone that could have recognized him. The square's name had changed to Place John Paul II, after the dead pontiff, yet regardless of title he finally felt he was someplace safe. The spot where he stood to the side of the square, between the great bronze equestrian statue of Charlemagne et ses leudes and the edge of the trees, was familiar to him, a constant in a world that was becoming increasingly tumultuous with amazing momentum.

Cameron had exited Place Dauphine as expediently as possible without breaking into a suspicious run. To elude authorities, he had crossed the square to the northern bank of Ile de la Cité and nearly run into oncoming traffic of emergency vehicles. Cameron did not want to be seen. Without hesitation, he veered away from the flashing lights and squawking sirens coming from mid-island. He continued his stride north along the sidewalk and away from the trail of first responders that were filing onto the avenue behind him. He made his way onto the Pont Neuf, the city's oldest bridge. He was about to cross the Seine when he heard the emergency squawks of additional vehicles rushing from the Paris Metro center. He doubled back to avoid being noticed. He followed the southern walk and at the first chance, slipped down the steps to continue along the Seine. Cameron kept moving toward the area of Ile de la Cité most infested with tourists.

Surrounded by tourists, Cameron was able to blend in almost seamlessly.

Cameron now stood safely in the shadow of the patina Olivier and Roland. The famed sword Durendal hovered above Cameron, eternally leading the Frank King Charlemagne and his warhorse Tencendor.

Cameron was reassured, yet this too reminded him of Pepe. Pepe Laroque, his friend of many years, more than a friend, a brother, now incinerated beneath the bursting plume of black smoke that poured skyward a short distance away.

Cameron had always been pleased by the mammoth sculpture, the representation of absolute power, of unification, of the good fight. Pepe referred to the magnificent work as a remnant of imperialism and, possibly worse, a recollection of a time when France and Germany were one. Pepe was, after all, a Frenchman.

Trained to fully be aware of his gear and surroundings, Cameron was unusually out of sorts. He had not taken the opportunity to regroup. The blade Pepe had given him was easily detected, heavy in his pocket, as were the Ruger and SIG tucked in his waist. Cameron reached inside the pocket of his sport coat. Another relieving autonomic breath pumped through his nose and into his chest. He had his mobile phone. His other belongings, and his friend, were lost in the explosion at the other end of Ile de la Cité.

The phone awoke with a full charge and reception. Cameron was thankful that he had powered the phone on the express train. That would mean–he patted the other breast of his coat and then searched inside that pocket–the charger was still with him, a small good thing. With his thumb, he zipped through the contacts to his restaurant Le Dragon Vert. Claude would assist him. Cameron tapped the screen and then held the phone to his ear. There was a series of clicks. Cameron imagined the signal being bounced against some satellite, and then the familiar ring. On the second ring, the other line picked up. Cameron spoke immediately, "Hello this is Cameron, I need to speak to—" the recorded voice of the restaurants hostess interrupted him. "Hello, thank you for calling Le Dragon Vert. Our hours are 10am to 11pm—" Cameron lowered the phone. The time difference from Paris to New York was six hours and the sun was high above the cathedral de Notre Dame. Stateside, Claude would be at the Union Square Greenmarket to greet the farmers and vendors as they set up.

Cameron slid his thumb down the screen to sort through the contacts again. He slipped too far into the letter R section. He went up the list to the first name, Claude Rambeaux and then double tapped the screen to make the connection.

"C'mon, Claude, pick up," said Cameron. He began to pace in a small circle.

On the third ring, Claude answered the phone, "Hello, this is Claude."

"Claude, this is Cameron."

Claude's voice elevated, "Cameron, I thought this was you. You are still away. The number was a bridge."

"I'm in Paris."

"Ah, Paris. I am at the Greenmarket, so beautiful. This morning I found some small aubergine to stuff."

Cameron lifted his chin. The words were a bit amiss. The events leading to this call were all too personal. "Listen," said Cameron. "Things are red right now."

Claude's tone became serious. The elation of a mere second before was lost. "What's wrong Cameron? How can I help you?"

"I am in danger," said Cameron. "I need to find somewhere safe."

"Where is Pepe?" asked Claude.

A punch of nausea landed in Cameron's inner gut as he mentally formed the words, yet to say them triggered a latent switch deep within him. "Pepe has fallen," said Cameron. He said the words in such a way that he was reporting matter of fact.

There was a pause.

"I see," said Claude. "You need the number for Absolon, correct?"

"The hotel in Asnières is the safest place I know right now," said Cameron.

"Do not worry," said Claude. "Make your way to the hotel, and I will make the call."

CHAPTER 53
ASNIÈRES, PARIS

So many years had passed for both Cameron and Asnières since his last visit, that he momentarily lost his bearing when he exited the metro station. Some of the buildings were the same. As with most old European cities, the eyesore flare-ups of modernization increase in relation to the distance from the city's metro center. Asnières was a suburb touched by such modernism. Convenience mart petrol stands, the bland architecture of new hotels, and anachronistic glass walled shopping centers peppered streets that held the generational homes he found familiar. He adjusted his mind to filter the transition of time, and then overlaid the Asnières before him, over the suburb of his younger days. The metro station, the pharmacy, and a few landmark buildings, now repurposed, led Cameron down a side street. He anticipated the old townhouse.

Cameron did not recognize the guesthouse until he was close, the facade disguised with newly coated stucco and partly hidden behind a lush floral garden. He may have continued past it, had the unique multi gabled frame not caught his eye.

The metal gate was the same, though there was no longer rust nor squeak. The fruit trees and slates of stone that composed the walkway were definitely a fresh part of the landscaped yard, as were the grape vines wrapped up and around the arbor trellis. The wooden door, no longer weatherworn, was a deep brilliant red, and partly open. Cameron gently pushed the door a bit further and then entered the foyer.

Cameron called out, "Bonjour, est quelqu'un à la maison? Is anyone home?"

"Un moment," came a younger man's voice from the back of the house.

The foyer also appeared foreign to Cameron, as did the adjoining library when he peeked further inside. The interior rooms had been renovated. Bright colors covered the once patina walls and some aged knick-knacks, none that Cameron recognized, peppered the few surfaces.

A thin mop haired man entered through the French doors from the opposite end of the library. The young man appeared boyish, though Cameron judged him to be near thirty. The man wore a Brown University sweatshirt and was wiping his hands with a cloth. He held out a hand, a slight hint of French in his English, "You must be Cameron."

Cameron was pleased Claude had eased his arrival. He smiled and took the man's hand. "Yes, that's right. I am looking for Absolon. Is he here?"

"That's me," said the young man.

"There is a mistake, I was looking—"

The young man finished Cameron's sentence, "For my grandfather, yes I know. I'm Abe—well, I am an Absolon too—I have always gone by Abe."

"Little Abe, yes of course, you have changed." Cameron hovered his hand waist level. "You have grown."

Abe lifted his brow, "Yes, that's true."

Cameron placed his hands on his hips. "Where is your

Daniel Arthur Smith

grandfather?" he asked.

"He is no longer with us."

"I'm sorry," said Cameron.

"Oh, that sounded wrong. Don't be sorry, he moved back to Algiers," said Abe. "He is very happy there."

"Oh."

"Yeah, I run the hotel now," said Abe. He gestured past Cameron. "Excuse me, may I?" Abe slipped past Cameron to the still open door. He leaned his head outside, and darted his eyes through the neighborhood. "Monsieur Claude said you might be followed."

"I don't believe I was," said Cameron. "Though I am not so sure it's safe to walk the Avenue des Champs-Élysées."

Comfortable that nothing past his garden was out of the ordinary, Abe closed the door and then headed back through the library. "Follow me to the garden, we can talk out there."

The French doors of the garden opened to a stone patio, shaded by a vine-covered pergola. Soft jazz and the pungent sweet scent of lilies permeated into the house. Bordering the patio were a variety of lilies, roses, and surrounding a corner arbor, similar to the one in the front of the house, a few groomed outcroppings of wildflowers. The simple courtyard and algae stained birdbath of Cameron's younger years had transformed to the lushness of a miniature estate.

On a low metal café table, a blue tin-serving tray emblazoned with a vibrant Orangina logo held a sweating bottle of sparkling lemonade and three tall glasses a lighter hue of blue than the tray. On a matching bench behind the small table sat an attractive young Asian woman, her blouse fully open, nursing a baby, easily no more than three months old. She did not appear modest or to mind the stranger entering the patio. She continued to serenely caress the suckling child, her tired eyes pleasant. Abe's mop of dark hair and disheveled attire mirrored the young mother. Cameron understood neither had been getting much rest.

Abe inhaled deeply and then in a soft voice introduced the young woman, "Cameron, this is my wife Kim."

Kim subtly lifted her head, her smile still pleasant, her caresses a natural repetition as the baby fed. Cameron was surprised by her American accent when she spoke. "It's really you, Cameron Kincaid, the Dragon Chef."

Cameron's eyes went wide. The events of the last few days had taken him far from the world he had created in New York.

"That's me," said Cameron. "Pleased to meet you. What is the little one's name?"

"This little hungry fella is Jonah," said Kim, "after my father. I love your shows. We only get one here. In Boston I used to watch you all of the time. Abe has told me many times you were a friend of the family. I didn't believe him."

"It's true, I knew Abe's grandfather quite well, and the family. You're American?"

Abe answered Cameron, "Kim and I met at Brown my sophomore year."

"My mother is Vietnamese and my father is from Massachusetts," said Kim. She gazed back down at the closed eyes of the babe in her arms. "And now little Jonah is French like his Daddy."

Cameron smiled a bit uncomfortably. "I'm intruding."

Kim raised her head again. "Not at all, sit. Abe, honey, pour Cameron a drink and tell him what you know."

"Thank you," said Cameron. He sat in one of the two metal patio chairs. Abe began to pour lemon seltzer into the three glasses. "So as I mentioned, Monsieur Claude explained to me why you are here." Cameron shifted his eyes to Kim, once again soothing her son. "Don't worry," said Abe. He offered Cameron the beverage and then took a seat in the second patio chair. "She knows what I know."

Cameron compressed his lips and then nodded.

Abe lifted his brow in a matter of fact fashion, then continued, "Well, anyway, I still know all of Absolon's friends."

"And Abe has few of his own," added Kim in a soft voice, now rocking back and forth.

"And I have a few of my own," nodded Abe. "So tracking down this Dada character was not that hard."

"You've found him already?"

"Not exactly. I am still waiting for friends to get back to me," said Abe.

"Hmm," said Cameron. He sipped the sparkling lemonade.

Abe grinned, "I did find out where he is going to be."

CHAPTER 54
8TH ARRONDISSEMENT OF PARIS

The leather jacket Cameron had borrowed from young Abe hugged his shoulders and upper arms tightly. The sheen of the blackened lambskin reflected the amber streetlamps with the same glow of the scooters and autos parked beside him. He flipped the enduro's kill switch and straightened himself, his legs spread wide to balance the motorbike in between. Without movement, the matching black helmet was becoming warm. He plucked his head from the snug heater rather than flip up the mask. He adjusted each driving glove, pulling down hard on the short cuffs and spreading his fingers wide to dig in deeply, and then, satisfied by the fit, flexed each hand. Uniform silhouettes of horse chestnut trees lined the roadways, already damp from the subtle evening mist, and muted beds of perennials filled the medians. The moist air, dense with the sweet pungent perfume of night blooming blossoms, enveloped him.

Cameron began to wait, gazing stone-faced at the restaurant across the street.

A short way ahead of him, the driver of the white

Bentley was also in waiting. Behind the white car, two silhouettes sat sentry in a small indigo Renault. Abe's friend had been correct. Dada was dining tonight at the Egyptian Room. Cameron pondered whether the warlord was undeterred by the earlier events of the day, confident the explosion that had killed Cameron's old friend would not trace back to him, or did Dada simply not care, disregarding the matter entirely. Cameron decided on the latter.

A faint drizzle had come, gone, and returned, still Cameron stayed in wait on the side of Rue Marbeuf. The hours of heavy traffic flooded across Avenue des Champs-Élysées at the end of the block. Taxis and town cars slipped past Cameron down the one-way street to let finely dressed guests arrive and depart from the trendy velvet roped restaurant, which, by this late hour, had transformed into a nightclub. Some of the guests he recognized from New York, some from his own restaurant. To go into the ultra art deco lounge of Egyptian Room would jeopardize his search for Dada. The risk of being recognized himself, even to have his name mentioned in a greeting, was far too great. Better to remain incognito in the partial shadow of the street, his back to approaching vehicles, no one looking back at the man on the motorbike, a common sight in Paris.

A few times, he was wary of Dada's men, twitching and fidgety in their seats. Once, Cameron thought he would need to move on when one of the large bodyguards stepped out of the Renault to stretch his legs. The man had stared a moment too long in Cameron's direction, an animal suspicious of his surroundings, instinctually drawn toward the predator. Distracted by the scolding of his colleague, the bodyguard stopped searching the night, and returned to his assigned post inside of the car. The man was not mistaken in that Cameron was a predator. No matter that he'd redefined himself as a debonair restaurateur, a worldly television personality. No matter how he lived his modern life day to day, Cameron Kincaid was and always would be a specialized commando, a man still utilizing an alias, no less than in the last years he'd served as a deep cover agent. The part of his psyche overwritten by intense training and conditioning would forever leave him an alpha of alphas, an apex predator.

Half past midnight, the bodyguard again removed himself from the Renault. This time the driver of the white Bentley also exited his vehicle. Both of the standing men pressed a finger to their ears. The driver of the Bentley opened a passenger door slightly. Dada was leaving the restaurant. Cameron slipped on his helmet in preparation. He reached down and switched the fuel line back on. When Dada, accompanied by two more suited bodyguards, made his way from Egyptian Room to the Bentley, Cameron lifted the motorbike upright by the handlebars. With the tip of his foot, he flipped the folded kick-start away from the bike. Once Dada and his men were in the vehicles and had begun to pull away, Cameron pounced on the kick-start to ignite the bike's engine. He did not want to draw the attention of the men in the Renault. He left the headlamp off, and only when the small motorcade was near the corner of Avenue des Champs-Élysées, did Cameron pull away from the curb.

The white Bentley and indigo Renault continued forward across Avenue des Champs-Élysées, Rue Marbeuf becoming Rue du Colisée. Cameron held the motorbike at the corner. The Arch de Triumph towered over Place Charles de Gaulle to his left and an even distance to his right was the Obélisque of Place de la Concorde. When the light began to change for the oncoming traffic, he popped the clutch to gun the enduro. The engine whined loudly, jetting the bike through the intersection no differently than a scurrying rat. After he crossed the busy avenue, he eased off the throttle and tapped back a gear. The bike disappeared again into the shadows. The motorcade was already to the busy Rue de Courcelles. This time Cameron did not make the light. Confident he would not lose Dada, he watched the motorcade gaining distance and waited. When the light did change, the taillights of the Renault disappeared to the right.

Cameron flicked his thumb to illuminate the bike's headlamp. To remain dark on these streets could attract unnecessary attention. He motored steady to the corner and then rolled onto Rue du Faubourg Saint-Honoré.

Dada had not travelled far. The Bentley and the Renault were at the valet station of the Hôtel Le Bristol. Cameron's stakeout had been a success. He had discovered Dada's Paris lair. Cameron was familiar with the hotel. He attended a birthday celebration there every year for an aging friend, a Francophile fragrance mogul from the States, and had stayed there on many other occasions in his new persona. How predictable that Ibrahim Dada would make his Paris home in yet another a five star hotel.

There was an issue. The staff of the Hôtel Le Bristol was familiar with Cameron as well. There would be no way he could walk in incognito as he and Pepe had through the service entrance of the May Fair. He would have to use another skillset to get to Dada.

The enduro leaned a hard left short of the hotel. Cameron rode around the block, stopping safely in the shadow of the first intersection past the hotel. The north side of the intersection was a good place to hide. If the Renault or Bentley were to leave the Hotel, they would be forced to turn south, a lower risk they would see him.

Cameron rested his helmet on the handlebars. He pulled his mobile phone from inside the leather jacket and dialed.

"Hello," said Abe.

"It's Cameron."

"Yeah, I saw that. Did you find him?"

"Your friend was right," said Cameron. "Not only was he at the restaurant, I was able to follow him to the Hôtel Le Bristol."

"Well, that's good," said Abe.

"Not exactly," said Cameron. "The last time I was in the Hôtel Le Bristol I was in the bar all night with U2."

"The band?"

"Yeah, the band."

"So they know you, got it, I have someone I can call," said Abe. "Give me a few minutes."

"No problem," said Cameron. "I'll be waiting right here. This time I'm not letting him out of my sight."

CHAPTER 55
HÔTEL LE BRISTOL, PARIS

The information from Abe's friend came by late afternoon. The suite that Ibrahim Dada had made his own was on the top floor of the Hôtel Le Bristol, the eighth floor, facing the garden. Near Cameron, two French paparazzi, each with a 500mm camera lens dangling from their belt, were discussing another guest of the hotel, a young pop star. Cameron circled the block again. Paparazzi stalking the young pop star were staked out at every exit. Cameron had to wait for the photo parasites to leave before he could approach the hotel.

Cameron's opportunity came where he most desired it, the service entrance to the adjacent Epicure restaurant. The new restaurant and terrace separated the hotel from the 1,200 square meter French garden and was perfect cover to get him close. The street clear, he ducked into the serviceway that ran between the gate and restaurant toward the hotel.

Hidden in the shadow of the columned pergola, Cameron peered across the terrace to the back wall of the hotel. The white Botticino marbled terrace was empty except for two white jacketed workers removing and folding the last of the cotton-linen tablecloths from the cast iron tables. He waited for them to finish before making his way to the back wall. As they folded the last tablecloth, he sized up the best point of access. The bubbling 'Fontaine aux Amours' fountain at the center of the terrace appeared to be his best opportunity.

The two began to chat and then one lit a cigarette. Cameron was prepared to wait out the pair. From inside the restaurant came a loud pop, the opening of a champagne bottle, followed by a beckoning shout. The smoker stomped out his cigarette and, with smiles on their faces, the two headed into the glass walled dining room. Bending at his waist, Cameron skirted the hedge to the fountain. The fountain was a bit farther from the first ledge than he had calculated, so he deduced he would need to climb to the top and launch himself onto the wall. From behind the fountain, he peeked back toward the glass walls of the Epicure restaurant. The two white jacketed men had gathered with three of the kitchen staff and were raising glasses. None of the indoor crew faced the fountain or the back of the hotel. Cameron counted to three then stair stepped up the base of the fountain, placed his hands on either side of the top basin and, in a hop, lifted his feet up near his hands.

In the odd pose of an arched cat, Cameron froze.

Across the terrace, hidden to him from beneath the pergola, was the hotel's grand garden, a magnificent array of tulips, daffodils, azaleas, rhododendrons, and facing Cameron, the gardener. The gardener was spraying water from a hose onto a bed of tulips, meters from the terrace. Focused on his ground level task, the gardener had not yet noticed Cameron, directly to his front.

Cameron remained a statue, a new fixture to the fountain. He had not expected to see a gardener watering so late in the evening. Then from within the restaurant came another shout. Cameron's eyes darted to the indoor crew. One of the white jacketed men was walking to a garden door. "Bastian," the man called out toward the gardener. The gardener's head jolted toward the restaurant. Cameron could see now the man was wearing headphones and, caught off guard, had jerked his head to the side without looking forward, to where Cameron crouched, breathless. The gardener smiled, began to roll his hose, and headed toward the door and the others.

Cameron waited until the crew again were raising glasses and then flung himself up and back to the ledge.

Cameron propelled himself to exactly where he needed to be to clutch the ledge above his head. He briefly hung to assess those celebrating meters away within the glass walls and then, confident he was clear, he swung his right hand over to lead his body around to face the wall. As soon as his hand made contact, he hoisted himself up and then onto the ledge.

Cameron's deltoids burned.

With stealth and speed, he wasted no time getting to the third floor, scaling his way to the suite's terrace. The scent of magnolias shot up from the French garden below. Cautiously, he maneuvered himself between windows to avoid detection. He carefully placed fingers and toes onto the ends of the ledges, gradually lifting himself above the surrounding skyline. Though he had not scaled a building in years, the effort was second nature. Countless missions in the eastern bloc had required subtle infiltration. There had been a mission in Prague where he found himself scaling up and down the same building several nights in a row, primarily for visits to the wife of a former Russian General he was converting to an asset.

Each grip from Cameron's hand, each push of his toe maneuvered him farther up the wall until he found himself below the terrace of Dada's suite. The room above was quiet. He spun his weight so that his back was again flat on the wall. Climbing as much mentally as physically, he already had his next move planned. His plan was to swing himself up onto the edge of the terrace. His deltoids still burned, yet he had blocked out the sensation. From his perch, he could see the sterile light and contrasting shadows of the hotel garden below and in the distance, the Basilica of the Sacré Cœur, the church of Saint-Augustin, and the rooftops of Paris.

Cameron filled his lungs with air and then, with a pounce of a cat practiced a thousand times before, flung himself up, around, and onto the ledge of the darkened terrace. He peered under the railing. The French doors were open, framed by sheer curtain panels that glowed back at him. There was no motion, no shadows against the interior lamp lit wall. He held firm on the ledge.

Cameron made ready the Ruger and then eased himself up and over the railing. With the greatness of stealth, he slowly moved toward the open door. His adrenalin intoxicating him, overriding the exhaustion of the day. He was a good adrenalin drunk.

Through the sheer curtain, Cameron inspected the room. The only light in the room emanated from a tall standing lamp in the far corner. At rest in a cushioned chair beside the lamp was Dada, silent; he appeared to be sleeping. Also from the room came a familiar smell that Cameron identified immediately, the reek of a bowel movement, the particular stench of a man that has recently passed.

Cameron moved into the room to have a better look.

Dada was sitting in the chair. Dada was not sleeping. His face was beaten and cut, his left ear was separated from his head, the shirt of his fine suit oozed with punch colored blood, his throat was slit across the entire base of his neck. Cameron recognized the cut as well as any signature.

"Pepe," said Cameron.

A dark shadow filled the doorframe to the adjoining

room, and then a figure came into the light.

On the chair before Cameron was a corpse that had been alive moments ago. Standing beside that corpse was a man, now alive, that had been dead.

"I knew you would come," said Pepe. "I could not wait."

CHAPTER 56
HÔTEL LE BRISTOL, PARIS

Pepe rested himself into a cushioned chair opposite the doorway from the freshly dead Ibrahim Dada. Already pumped with adrenalin, a confused wave of emotion coursed into Cameron. His old friend, a fellow Green Dragon, the man he had counted on through countless missions, was alive. Cameron was elated to see his brother-in-arms, yet the carved up warlord across the room, the work of his friend, was jarring. He peered at the dead man, mentally recreating the slow death. Cameron had seen men killed in this fashion many times before, and certainly he had no remorse for the evil tyrant. But Pepe had been extreme. He had tortured Dada, beat him, and then slit his throat. He had not cut from behind by surprise, rather coldly from the front.

"You were looking him in the eyes," said Cameron, fixed on the glazed sightless orbs staring out to nothing.

Pepe had reclaimed a bit of the jolliness that had fallen from him the past few days. "I wanted him to see me as I took his future from him."

"I reject the glamour of evil," said Cameron.

"Do not quote verse to me, brother," said Pepe. "I

have finally found Christine."

Cameron shifted his full attention to Pepe. "You have?" Cameron peered into the adjoining room. "She is here?"

"No."

"You know where she is?"

"I know much more than that. Sit. Sit."

Cameron dropped himself onto a wooden chair on the far side of the French doors, resting his hands, still holding the Ruger, on his lap. The exhaustion was beginning to take a toll on him. "The others, the bodyguards?"

"They are in the other room. I did not need them," said Pepe.

"So what happened? How are you—"

"Alive?" said Pepe. "I was going to the window to call down to you to ask the restaurant for some, um, what is the word for miel?"

"Honey."

"Oui, to get some honey. I saw Rudy from the restaurant offering you the box and wine. I looked to the table and thought very quickly. I ran to the door and was at the second floor when, boom."

"The explosion," said Cameron.

"Yes, the explosion came," said Pepe. "When I reached the gallery, I entered the cellar and then left through the sewer. I did not know if anyone was waiting in Place Dauphine so I thought better if I appeared to have died."

"Well, that worked," said Cameron. "How did you end up here?"

"Probably the same as you. On a hunch, I called my contact back in Montreal. He told me of a bar where Somali frequent. I went to the bar and waited. The barman told me the men that work with Dada came in every night when they are in town. I gave the man some euros and began to drink. I guess I drank a bit more than I planned. By late afternoon, some men came in and the barman gave me a signal. I watched the men until they left and then followed them. I peeled one away and hauled him below to the catacombs."

Cameron was unsure where Pepe's story was going. Pepe continued.

"I had a discussion with the man and could not convince him to tell me where Dada was staying. Then I realized the man's comrades had followed me into the catacombs and he was simply stalling me for time, so in the dark I killed them one by one until I got to the last man," said Pepe.

"And he told you Dada was here," said Cameron.

"He was easy to convince. Pepe reached into the pocket of his jacket and removed a fistful of something. He tossed what he held onto the floor for Cameron to see in the light. Cameron's eyes widened, his mind reeled. Pepe, without changing his tone, continued his story.

"I presented the last man with the ears of his colleagues. He was quick to tell me where to find his general."

"Hmm, I see," said Cameron, not wanting to believe what Pepe was saying.

"Then I came here and waited. Dada told me what I wanted to know and more."

"What did he say?"

"Listen for yourself," said Pepe. Pepe reached into an inside pocket and then tossed Cameron what he had found there. Cameron caught the small piece of electronics. He examined the digital recorder and then hit play.

Dada's pain immediately spouted from the tinny recording. Cameron sighed and continued to listen.

Dada screaming: "What are you doing? You are crazy."

Next came the sharp crack of a slap, followed by another, Dada screaming with each blow.

Dada beginning to whimper: "What do you want. I did nothing."

Pepe: "You know what you did. Now tell me!"

Another cracking sound cut through the recording, followed by another tinny and muted howl from Dada.

Pepe again, determined: "You hijacked the Kalinihta, now where is the girl?" another crack, "Where is my sister?"

Dada: "I did not do this. I let them stay at the compound and sent along some men."

Pepe: "That was your compound? Answer me," slap, slap. Cameron peered up at the bloody corpse in the chair, the bruising that had begun on the sides of the face, and the bruising that had ceased after death.

Dada: "Why should I tell you? You are a dead man."

Pepe: "Because I will cut this from your body."

Dada: "You will do no such, Aaaaaa! You are dead! You are dead!"

Pepe: "I may be dead, but I am a dead man with a knife."

Dada: "Yes, that was my compound. The plan was for him to hide until you came. Then his father would be happy to deal."

Pepe: "What are you saying? That Nikos was in on this?"

Dada: "Yes, Nikos, this was his plan to push his father Demetrius into a deal for a cut of the profit. This was his plan."

Pepe: "His plan?"

Dada: "Nikos said that if Christine were captured that you would ride in like the cavalry to rescue her. The kidnapping was a setup. All planned by Nikos."

Pepe: "And you took Christine in return?"

Dada: "No! I know nothing about her!"

Pepe screamed: "You lie! You lie!" along with repetitive slaps, screams, and moans.

Dada: "No, no. This was his plan from the beginning. Go to Gstaad and ask him yourself. Nikos Stratos. No! No! Stop this! You are a dead man!!"

Cameron stopped the recording and peered into Pepe's

satiated eyes.

~*~

CAMERON KINCAID RETURNS IN
THE SOMALI DECEPTION
EPISODE IV

~*~

ABOUT THE AUTHOR

Daniel Arthur Smith is the author of the international bestsellers *THE CATHARI TREASURE, THE SOMALI DECEPTION,* and a few other novels and short stories.

He was raised in Michigan and graduated from Western Michigan University where he studied meta-physics, cognitive science, philosophy, and comparative religion. He began his career as a bartender, barista, poetry house proprietor, teacher and then became a technologist and futurist for the Fortune 100 across the Americas and Europe.

Daniel has traveled to over 300 cities in 22 countries, residing in Los Angeles, Kalamazoo, Prague, Crete, and now writes in Manhattan where he lives with his wife and young sons.

For more information, visit **danielarthursmith.com**

STAY IN THE LOOP

Following your favorite authors on Facebook, Twitter, or other social media has become a sketchy business. Facebook and other companies block authors from conversing regularly with readers unless they are willing to cough up BIG BUX to 'promote' every post. To make sure you are receiving the latest updates, freebies, and stories on everything in the Daniel Arthur Smith universe you have to join his email newsletter. As a subscriber, you'll receive early Advance Review Copies (ARCS) of all of Daniel's books and stories… for free! In addition to all of that, Daniel regularly gives away lots of other loot like signed books and posters, so make certain that you are subscribed.